Ned Visits Food Land

Debora A. Robinett, R.D.

Dedication

This book is dedicated to my three children, Rachelle, Jason, and Jesse, who provided me the inspiration and encouragement to bring Ned's valuable message of whole-food, plant-based eating to all children and their loving caregivers.

Meet Ned.

He lives with his mom and dad in the city.

Ned's mom and dad work hard all day and when it's time to eat, they buy their food at the grocery store.

Most of the food they buy is already made and sold in boxes, cans and bags.

Ned thinks all food comes from the store.

One day, Ned's Aunt Milly invites him to visit her and his cousin at her farm in the country.

Ned's mom and dad say it is OK.

Aunt Milly travels to the city on the
train to meet Ned and takes him to the farm.

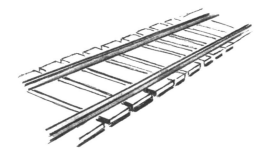

Ned loves the train ride.

He sees so many new things along the way.

Ned loves Aunt Milly's
farm even more.
Ned and his cousin Amanda
get to feed all the
farm animals.

They gather eggs from the chickens,
help milk the cows, pick fruit from the trees
and the vegetables from the garden.

Ned even sees the bees making honey.

Aunt Milly shows Ned how to clean the vegetables and make colorful, tasty meals.

Ned can't believe how good everything tastes.

After dinner, the scraps of leftovers are saved for the soup pot, fed to the animals or taken to the compost pile.

There are no boxes, cans or glass containers to take to the garbage can.

Ned and Amanda love
working together on
the farm and playing
outside in the fresh air
and sunshine.

Ned feels strong
and happy.

He even looks different.

Sadly, it is time for Ned to go home.

So Aunt Milly and Ned leave the farm
and take the train back to the city.

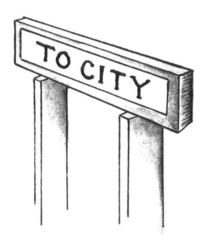

Ned is sad to say goodbye to his
cousin Amanda and to the farm
but promises to come back again soon.

But even though Ned misses the farm,
he misses his mom and dad and
can't wait to tell them everything
he saw at the farm.

Ned's first day home, he shows his mom and dad
where the fresh food is along the sides
of their store and that Aunt Milly told him
about the Farmer's Market where
only fresh fruits and vegetables are sold.

Ned finds the same
food at their store that
he saw at the farm.

Everything was fresh.

Ned even remembered
to bring a shopping
bag from home.

Ned helps in the kitchen and shows his mom and dad how to make fresh meals.

They are surprised how easy it is and that they saved money buying fresh food.

And that's how Ned's family kept shopping and eating.
Ned hopes that you can visit a farm someday
but if you can't, you can still find and...

eat fresh fruits and vegetables every day.

Debora Robinett, M.A., R.D., C.D., is the President of the Health Enhancement Corporation and has spent more than 30 years in her nutrition practice teaching useful strategies and practical skills for happy, healthy eating and living.

Her mantra is functional health. Habits integrate with your lifestyle for improved everything.

Feathers in her cap include television appearances on New Day Northwest, and interviews with The Wall Street Journal, Bicycling, Fitness and Therapy Times. She has taught college nutrition courses as well as served on the board of the Greater Seattle Dietetic Association.

A Pacific Northwest native, Debora is also an avid golfer, skier, traveler, involved community leader, aspiring beekeeper-owner of Eden's Honey, and mother of three. Her daughter has gone on to work in wellness too, inspired by Debora's way of teaching nutrition which is inspiring, accessible, full of color, and endlessly fascinating. Perhaps she was also inspired by Ned, who Debora dreamed up during her nutrition internship as a way to teach healthy eating habits to children.

Food Color Swatches

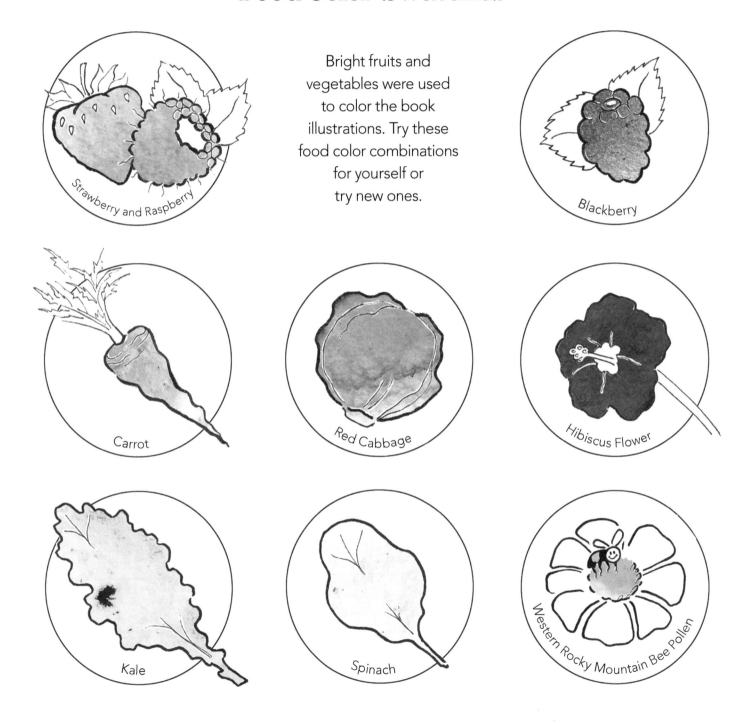

Strawberry and Raspberry

Blackberry

Bright fruits and vegetables were used to color the book illustrations. Try these food color combinations for yourself or try new ones.

Carrot

Red Cabbage

Hibiscus Flower

Kale

Spinach

Western Rocky Mountain Bee Pollen

Food Color Swatches

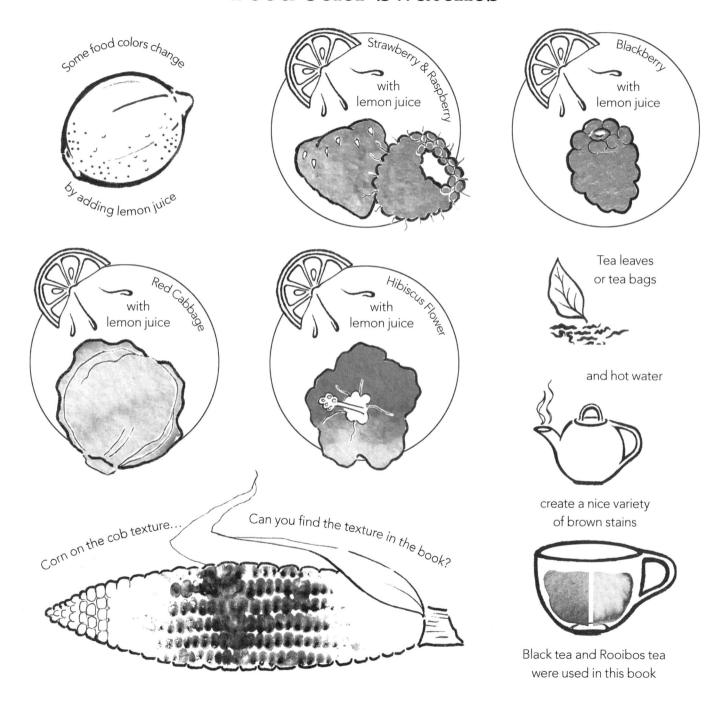

Some food colors change by adding lemon juice

Strawberry & Raspberry
with lemon juice

Blackberry
with lemon juice

Red Cabbage
with lemon juice

Hibiscus Flower
with lemon juice

Tea leaves or tea bags

and hot water

create a nice variety of brown stains

Black tea and Rooibos tea were used in this book

Corn on the cob texture... Can you find the texture in the book?

CPSIA information can be obtained
at www.ICGtesting.com
Printed in the USA
LVHW070908310119
605889LV00041B/508/P